W9-BWF-599

For Doodle, who fears not — L. G.-B.

For my family — B. L.

Second edition 1997

Library of Congress Catalog Card Number 95-71366

ISBN 0-7636-0343-0

2 4 6 8 10 9 7 5 3 1

Printed in Hong Kong

This book was typeset in Maiandra.
The pictures were done in watercolor and pen and ink.

Candlewick Press
2067 Massachusetts Avenue
Cambridge, Massachusetts 02140

SAY BOO!

Lynda Graham-Barber

illustrated by Barbara Lehman

CANDLEWICK PRESS
CAMBRIDGE, MASSACHUSETTS

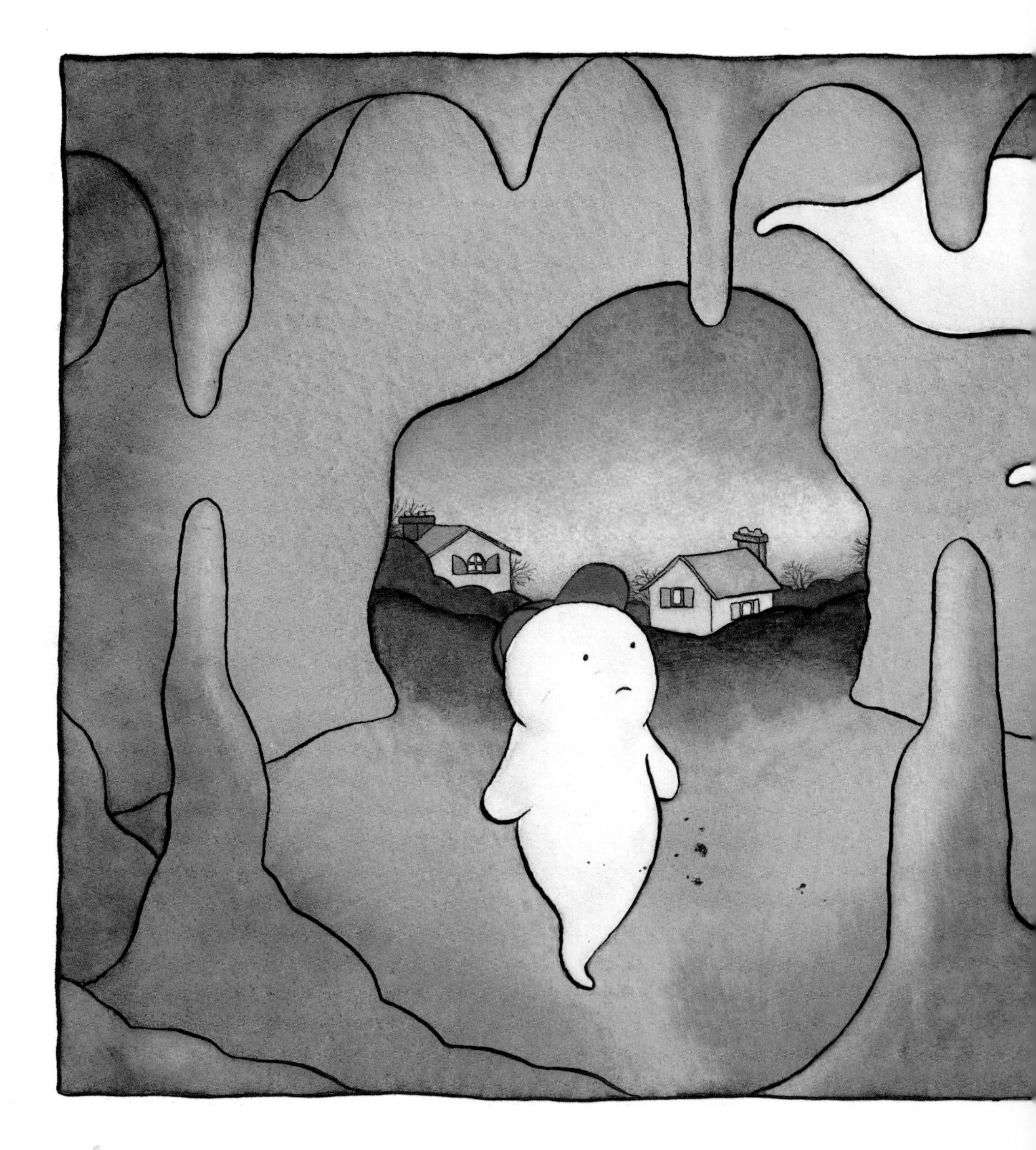

Ben watched his brothers and sisters swoop through the cave, shrieking and howling. But he didn't join them.

All week long, Ben had stood in front of the mirror, puckering his lips. As hard as he tried, the little ghost couldn't say "Boo."

Who's ever heard of a ghost who can't say "Boo"? he thought.

With a whoosh, Ben's brother Boris landed beside him. "C'mon, Ben," he said. "Tonight's Halloween and you haven't even scared anyone yet."

"I know," Ben said with a sigh.

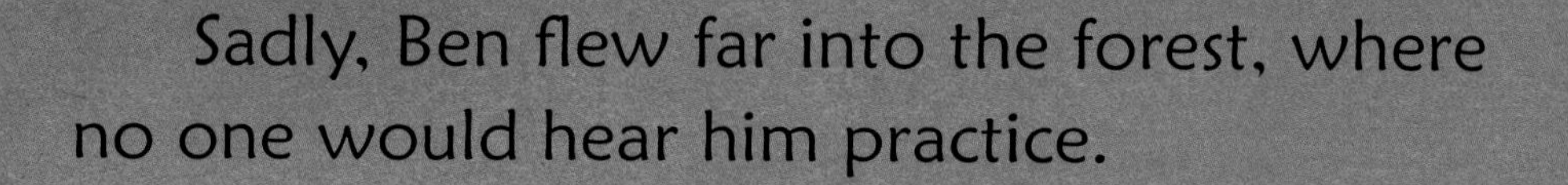

Sadly, Ben flew far into the forest, where no one would hear him practice.

He sat in a tree, took a deep breath, and puckered his lips. "Whooo!" Ben's voice bounced off the tall pine trees.

"Whoo-whoo, yourself," said a high, clear voice. Ben looked up and saw a large owl sitting on a branch. "Owls say 'Whoo,'" said the owl. "You're supposed to say 'Boo.'"

"I know," Ben said, and he flew out of the forest and into a meadow, where he tried again.

Ben took a deep breath, puffed up his chest, and puckered his lips. "Mooo!" he bellowed.

“Moo-moo, yourself,” said a low, deep voice. Peering at Ben through the lush green grass was a cow. “Cows say ‘Moo,’” it said. “You’re supposed to say ‘Boo.’”

"I know," Ben said. *I'll never be a scary Halloween ghost*, he thought. Ben flew off and came to a long stone bridge. There he stopped, took his deepest breath ever, and puckered his lips. "Cooo!" he wailed.

"Coo-coo, yourself," came a soft, sweet voice. A bird in a nest under the bridge ruffled its feathers and said, "Doves say 'Coo.' You're supposed to say 'Boo.'"

"It's no use," Ben said and began to cry.

Ben flew back to the forest, crying. Suddenly, a brown bat swooped down and landed on his shoulder.

"Boo-hoo, boo-hoo," the bat mocked. "What's this — a scary ghost crying on Halloween?"

"Boo-hoo, yourself," Ben mumbled. "Boo-hoo, boo-hoo, boo — Hey! I said 'Boo'!" he shouted. "Boo! Boo! Boo!"

"Eek!" squeaked the bat, and he flew off, trembling.

"Boo-boo, scaredy-bat!" Ben shouted after him.

Boo!
Boo!
Boo!
Boo!
Boo!
Boo!
Boo!
Boo!

Boo!

That Halloween night, when Ben joined Boris and all the other ghosts, his “Boo” was the scariest of all!